l a u r e n   c h i l d

I am NOT sleepy and I WILL NOT go to bed

CANDLEWICK PRESS

A special thank-you to Mrs. Fish at Big Fish
and hello to Little Fish

For the supremely stylish,
and fantastically fabulous,

Sandro and Piera

**with love from
Lauren**

Perry

For Perry with a
squillion thanks for a
zillion favors

(p.s. i hope this typeface isn't a style crime.)

First U.S. paperback edition 2005
Library of Congress Cataloging-in-Publication Data is available.
Library of Congress Catalog Card Number 00-066682
ISBN 978-0-7636-1570-3 (hardcover) / ISBN 978-0-7636-2970-0 (paperback)
First published in Great Britain in 2001 by Orchard Books, London
13 12
WKT 10 9
Printed in Shenzhen, Guangdong, China
This book was typeset in Officina Serif Book and Badloc.
The illustrations were done in mixed media.
Designed by Anna-Louise Billson
Candlewick Press, 99 Dover Street, Somerville, MA 02144
visit us at www.candlewick.com

I have this little sister, Lola.
She is small and very funny.
Sometimes I have to keep an eye on her.
Sometimes Mom and Dad ask me to try and
get her off to bed.
This is a hard job
because Lola likes to stay up late.

Lola likes to stay up coloring

and

scribbling

and

sticking

and

wriggling

and
bouncing
chattering.
and most of all

Usually, when I say,
    "Lola, Mom says it is time for bed,"
    she says,
    "No! I am NOT sleepy and

                    I
                    WILL
                    NOT
                    go to bed."
                         I say,

                    "But all the birds
                        have gone to sleep."

She says,
    "But I am **not** a bird,
        Charlie."

"But you must be slightly sleepy, Lola,"
I say.

Lola says,
"I am not slightly sleepy at 6

or 7

or 8

and I am still
wide awake at 9

and not at all tired at 10

11

12

and I will probably still be perky at **even** **13** O'CLOCK in the morning."

Lola says she **never** gets tired.

One night I said, "But if there's no bedtime, there can be no bedtime drink, and it's pink milk tonight."

(Lola really likes pink milk.)

"Are you sure you don't want to go to bed?"

"But Charlie," says Lola, "if I have pink milk,
the tigers will want pink milk too."
"Tigers?" I ask. "What tigers?"
                    "The tigers at the table, Charlie.
They are waiting for their bedtime drink.
       Tigers get very cross if they have to wait."

So I make pink milk

for Lola and three tigers.

Then I say,
"Let's go and brush our teeth."

So Lola says, "But Charlie, I can't brush my teeth because somebody is using my toothbrush."
"But who would use your toothbrush?" I ask.
Lola says, "I think it's that lion. I saw a lion with my toothbrush and now he's brushing his teeth with it."
"But isn't this your toothbrush, Lola?" I ask.
"Oh," says Lola, "he must be using yours."

So Lola and one lion

brush their teeth.

Then I say, "You have to take
a bath. You look a bit grubby."
"Who says?" says Lola.
"Mom does," I say. "She's coming
to check in **one** minute."
And then what do you think Lola says?
"But Charlie, I can't have a bath
because of the whales."
"What whales?"
I ask,
looking
around.

Bubble Cat

Bubble Bath

"The whales swimming in
the bathtub. They're taking up all
the room," she says.
"Well, what do you want me
to do about it?" I ask.
"Maybe you will have to help me
shoo **one** of them down
the drain," says Lola.
So I help Lola shoo
    one
      whale
        down
          the
            drain.

And
then
Lola
hops
into
the
tub.

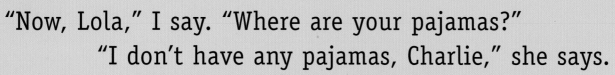

"Now, Lola," I say. "Where are your pajamas?"

"I don't have any pajamas, Charlie," she says.

I say, "What about these under your pillow?"

"Those are not my pajamas," says Lola, shaking her head.

"Oh, no. Those pajamas belong to two dancing dogs."

"Well, do you think they would let you just borrow their pajamas?" I ask.

"Maybe," says Lola.
"But you will
have to call them on
the telephone and ask."

"They say the pajamas suit you better than them.
You can wear them whenever you like."

And so Lola
gets into
her pajamas.

At last
Lola is ready for bed and I say,

"Now, Lola,
I have given three **tigers**
their pink milk

and

watched a **lion**
use my toothbrush

and

shooed one
whale
down
the
drain

and

telephoned two
dancing dogs
about pajamas.

NOW

will

you

please

hop

into

bed."

Lola says,
"Yes, yes, Charlie.
I'm hopping,
I'm hopping . . ."

"But I think there's one in **yours**," says Lola, as she snuggles under her covers.

"Good night, Charlie.
Good night, Hippopotamus."